Temporary Euphoria

A Poetry Book by
Hugo Jepsen

Chapters

Preface

When one falls in love for the first, a temporary feeling of euphoria hits the hearts of those involved in it.

A parallel vision and sentiment of fairytale-likeness upon the world is shed. And you believe you'll love them forever and ever until reality hits. However, no matter how time passes — that's always going to be your first love.

This edition contains 12 original poems and 5 bonuses.

Enjoy it,
Hugo Jepsen

Euphoria

I will rather be with myself
over being with somebody else -
always, something that feels forever,
yet, I still rather pursue it over being together.

Don't tell me, I'm wrong when I'm not,
don't tell me you fantasize about
the person who can never be yours -
too much trouble for something you can't run for.

But tell me if you've had any odd days
which everything you want to do
and everything else you want to say,
gets trapped, for some reason, inside of you.

But the best feeling in the world -
I dreamt of it as euphoria, even though,
some people say that it's not it, it's love
I couldn't disagree more on that, so.

Human

If I could pause my heart -
I would do so, right now.
But holding my breath,
it's all that this is about.

If you want me to be
the number one on your phone -
I'm not sure if that one will be me -
lately but lately, I rather am alone.

You think that I could do this,
you think that I could that,
but if you forget, I'm human
and that I've been stabbed in the back.

But if I could - baby - if I could,
I'd be of metal, I'd be a machine -
I'd never be living, I'd never die,
I would be just about everything.

Streets

The way you look at me
and the way I feel your touch,
I just feel like it's a good time to die -
can't deviate my look from your eyes.

Every time I walk in your streets -
whilst we held hands - felt so shy -
when I decided to fall in love,
I never thought of this love's size.

But your streets have gone your quiet,
they were stolen by my loneliness -
where once screams were heard,
now, it's just a resting place of my happiness.

Why the distance gotta be so hard?
I've done everything to pull us closer,
but after you saw my hidden scars,
closeness became scary in my heart.

Understandable

I had a dream and if I -
if I can be honest,
it seemed like a nightmare,
if you still want to care.

When I wake up and I see
that you're not here with me -
I feel like my skin is burning,
but I can't change a damn thing.

I tried to scream but I was underwater,
it might not be what you want to hear,
but it seems I have everything I wanted.

You promised you'd be kind,
you promised you'd never lie
but I guess it was your lie on its own -
only understandable when one
prefers to be alone.

Relationships

I hold no grudges, no promises
to whom has promised me the world,
because trusting might get me hurt -
scared of everything, scared of love.

It's time to pull our weapons on the ground,
it's time that we call this relationship quits -
I don't know - I don't know what to do about
something that I want but it's not healthy for me.

I gather memories like I keep an eye on your soul -
your mind is all but a story that keeps me entertained,
and your heart is nothing like hearts I've ever known.

And if I ever compliment something you don't wear,
it might mean that I'm keeping my eye on you,
because I'm innocently curious about the things you like to do.

The Fairytale begins...

Her Majesty

Sometimes you call me under -
but under is where I don't want to be,
I'd give up my simple life
to become your only queen.

It seems like she has anything she wants
because her love is a temporary high
and when you're running towards her,
she seems to be running even faster.

And if she can keep you warm
when I'm not there to revive
the dead parts of your body -
I appreciate her in your life.

I agree that her hands touch the sky
when one wants to be sixty feet in the ground,
but please tell me that you won't betray me,
I might not be able to touch the sky, but I'm here now.

Whispered Hunter

It seems like her madness
can hide anywhere she wants
and if only that could bring you happiness,
I'd let her have you anytime she wanted.

Your body runs cold without my presence
but if she comes near you, you warm up instantly -
so why don't you warm up when it's me?

If you throw knives at my queue
I'll be the one throwing them back at you.
You better run when I'm chasing my dreams,
I've become the hunter of whispers whom I'm meant to be.

When we first met, our hearts
experienced a temporary lie -
but her love - her love
is your permanent high.

Abusive Angel

Something about your soul
feels soft as if I'm touching an angel -
but at the reverie of the night,
you become the beast of my sights.

If I ask you to let it snow,
would you let me know?
Something about your powers seduces
the soul of mine and that's quite abusive.

I keep forgetting - there's no love in the air -
something about me and you isn't fair.
I don't know think I know myself
without relying on your help.

I hate it when I fall for your fruit of love -
these are my own humble clothes,
this is how I show up to the world
without fear of once more getting hurt.

The Fairytale dissipates...

Disguise

I never left you cold in the night -
I scream for fairies to come for help,
but lies have always been knives
disguised as good and pure men.

I know that if you take the train,
you'll come right back to my home -
and that's why I need to let you live
your life as if you were born alone.

There are many things that I know
that it can never be known -
if I let you know all my secrets,
it's a free ticket inside my soul.

And my little angel on my shoulder
disguised as a devil - full of himself -
has told me that if I let somebody in,
it's another free passage to let me be killed.

Cursed

It seems it's a bit cold tonight -
would you hold the palm of my hand?
I wish I could you tell the secrets
that keep me warm but I can't.

If you knew that his love
was magnificently cursed -
I bet you'd stay even more
and that is not allowed -
can't let my hurt become love.

Spring breaks loose
as love brings fear -
I'd live this moment
over and over until I die
instead of miserable become.

I let your flowers bloom
and now I'm covered in you -
that's why you win and I lose.

Hold Hands

I am staying at my parents' house,
but all the roads I take remember me of you
and then, I remember how much I miss my hometown.

Time flies at the mercy of healing wounds -
but I wouldn't be healing if I were with you -
that's why doctors say we should be apart
even if that is what's breaking my heart.

I wonder about which people I can trust -
it's hard to tell, it's hard to picture a soul,
if I can rely on feelings that hurt
to leave the comfort I've never known.

But I still stayed over and on the porch,
watching the myriads of rain particles fall,
I wish you'd be here so you could hold my hand
and if the world ends right now, I'd be happy then.

Cold Blood

Rain is pouring down
and I look out the window
thinking, 'what should I do now?'.

I've fooled so many people
with engagement in mystery -
my life is part of that history.

I lie and say I'm better on my own,
playing hide and seek in the snow,
with nothing but books and things I know -
because the unknown is outside of me being alone.

And then cold was my best friend -
tears flooded and cold-blooded, it's the new me -
so I can never let myself fall in love even if I want to be.

Bonus

you don't know listen because you know everything

You don't allow anybody
to speak but instead -
you call me out in the night,
saying you can't get to bed.

What did you say?
You don't listen
because you know everything.
It's how you tell me to love you
because of the things you've been through.

I believe we have chemistry,
I can feel all over your energy
but that doesn't mean that
we should get back together
and forget the misfortunes of the past.

If one day, you find me close to cry,
it's because I quench for freedom -
to fight the darkness, I cry for light.

Delicacy

Delicacies taste like a daydream -
hell, on the other hand, might sharp skin
on those who continue to commit sins.

As if the vessels sketching their teeth
are biting, biting their mouthful lips -
yet, they scatter their life lessons in whips.

Why cannot one be kind to just be?
Why do they have to correct
all the good acts born inside of me?

I wonder but that's the only thing I do,
courage lacks in the back of my throat,
so I can never tell them what I feel is true.

Care For Me

I try to let down my guard
but I still want to hide my scars -
Why it's got to be this hard,
just to open slightly my heart?

Don't tell me a damned word
if you don't believe in it -
but if you ever dare to love me,
I'd be - I'd just be happy.

Even if I tell you that we might -
it might be better to just deny
everything and keep me on the run
because it's easier to not let me get burnt.

Don't say it's easy to just let go
when you can ever let go of
the heartbreak that you already know.

Don't say it's easy to open-up
when all you know is how to break up.
So don't tell me you love if you don't dare
to tell me how much you truly, for me, care -
and it's not that I don't care, it's just I'm scared.

Never Truthful

Tell me all that I wanna hear
before you do your magic and disappear.
Tell me whether it feels sweet to you
or if when you lie, just feels good.

Why do I never tell the truth?
You think it's easier for me not to
fall out of love if you ever do.

But I would fall harder if you could
tell me why you're always coming to my home.
And then, I would but I really would
consider if being with you is better than being alone.

Because that's what love means -
that's what love means to me.

I fell out of love

If you give me love -
it needs to be every day -
I promise you won't get hurt.

If you find speechless
of many things to say,
it's because I don't
want to be awake.

I find it hard to answer
questions which I
don't know the answer to -
I just know, I fell out of love with you.

Copyrights

Credits

The book was written by Hugo Jepsen, edited by Hugo Jepsen, Illustrated by Hugo Jepsen and Published by Amazon Kindle Publishing.

Disclaimer

Any resemblance with other content out there is pure coincidence. This book is one hundred per cent original and based on real-life and life events.

www.ingramcontent.com/pod-product-compliance
Lightning Source LLC
Chambersburg PA
CBHW080732120726
48001CB00010B/3202